DISCOVE
ANCIENT CIVILIZA

THE ANCIENT
EGYPTIANS

David West

Gareth Stevens
PUBLISHING

Please visit our website, www.garethstevens.com.
For a free color catalog of all our high-quality books,
call toll free 1-800-542-2595 or fax 1-877-542-2596.

Cataloging-in-Publication Data

Names: West, David.
Title: The ancient Egyptians / David West.
Description: New York : Gareth Stevens Publishing, 2017. | Series: Discovering ancient civilizations | Includes index.
Identifiers: ISBN 9781482450675 (pbk.) | ISBN 9781482450699 (library bound) | ISBN 9781482450682 (6 pack)
Subjects: LCSH: Egypt–Civilization–To 332 B.C.–Juvenile literature. | Egypt–Antiquities–Juvenile literature.
Classification: LCC DT61.W47 2017 | DDC 932–dc23

First Edition

Published in 2017 by
Gareth Stevens Publishing
111 East 14th Street, Suite 349
New York, NY 10003

Copyright © 2017 David West Books

Designed by David West Books

Photo credits: P23, Pataki Márta

Printed in the United States of America

CPSIA compliance information: Batch #CS16GS: For further information contact Gareth Stevens, New York, New York at 1-800-542-2595.

DISCOVERING
ANCIENT CIVILIZATIONS

THE ANCIENT
EGYPTIANS

David West

Gareth Stevens
PUBLISHING

CONTENTS

Ancient Egyptians were ruled by a pharaoh

The civilization of ancient Egypt lasted more than three thousand years, from the first **dynasty** in 3,100 BC to around 30 BC, when Cleopatra died.

The success of ancient Egyptians was due to the rich fertile land along the edges of the Nile River. Most ancient Egyptians worked as farmers, craftsmen and scribes. A small group of people were nobles and at the opposite end of the social scale were slaves. These different groups of people made up the population.

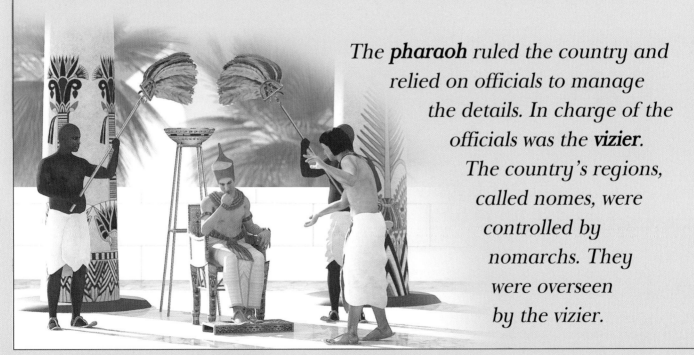

*The **pharaoh** ruled the country and relied on officials to manage the details. In charge of the officials was the **vizier**. The country's regions, called nomes, were controlled by nomarchs. They were overseen by the vizier.*

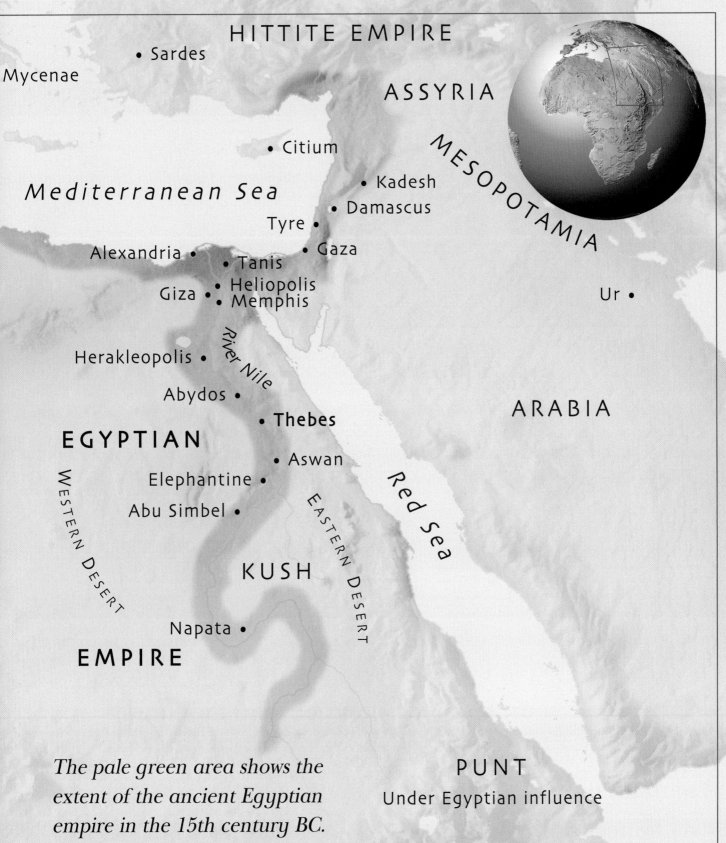

HITTITE EMPIRE

• Sardes

Mycenae

ASSYRIA

MESOPOTAMIA

• Citium

Mediterranean Sea

• Kadesh
• Damascus

Tyre •

Alexandria •   • Gaza

• Tanis

Giza • • • Heliopolis
      • • Memphis

Ur •

Herakleopolis •

River Nile

Abydos •

ARABIA

EGYPTIAN

• Thebes

• Aswan

Elephantine •

Abu Simbel •

WESTERN DESERT

EASTERN DESERT

Red Sea

KUSH

Napata •

EMPIRE

The pale green area shows the extent of the ancient Egyptian empire in the 15th century BC. The darker areas are where the people lived.

PUNT
Under Egyptian influence

7

The ancient Egyptians loved hunting

Hunting in Egypt was reserved for rich nobles. It was a sport for kings, **courtiers** and **dignitaries**. Hunting was important to the ancient Egyptians for many reasons. As well as providing meat and skins it was a chance for the hunters to prove their **prowess**.

When they hunted in the desert the pharaoh and his companions would gallop after their prey in chariots.

Lions were hunted with arrows, fired from a speeding chariot. In a single year, the pharaoh Amenhotep III killed more than one hundred lions.

Hunts took place in the marshes too, for birds and fish—and even for the chance to kill a hippopotamus.

A marsh hunter would use a decoy bird to lure a waterfowl close and a throwing stick to bring it down.

Farmers farmed on the banks of the Nile River

 The soil in Egypt was very fertile. This was because every year the fields were flooded by the Nile River. When the floodwaters went down there would be a fresh layer of mud which was excellent soil for plants to grow in after it had been plowed.

The Egyptians grew a variety of crops such as barley

A farmer plows the soil while another sows seeds behind him. A child throws stones to keep the birds away. Geese are herded to safety.

to make beer, wheat to make bread, pulses, beans, lentils, onions, garlic, radishes, lettuce and parsley. **Papyrus** and flax were also grown for many uses.

Fruit was also grown. Grapes, watermelon, figs, olives, apples and pomegranates were all part of the ancient Egyptian's diet.

The pharaoh was head of the army

Soldiers of the Egyptian army were recruited from the general population. The army also employed **mercenaries** from Nubia, Kush and Libya. The soldiers were armed with spears, axes, maces and a curved sword called a khopesh. Bows and arrows were the main projectile weapons. For protection they carried wooden shields covered in hide.

The pharaoh, wearing a blue helmet, shouts encouragement from his chariot as his army charges towards the enemy.

Chariots were used in large numbers to support the main body of the army, which was made up of infantry. On rare occasions the pharaoh would lead the army into battle.

Lions were trained to run alongside the pharaoh's chariot and attack enemy soldiers in battle.

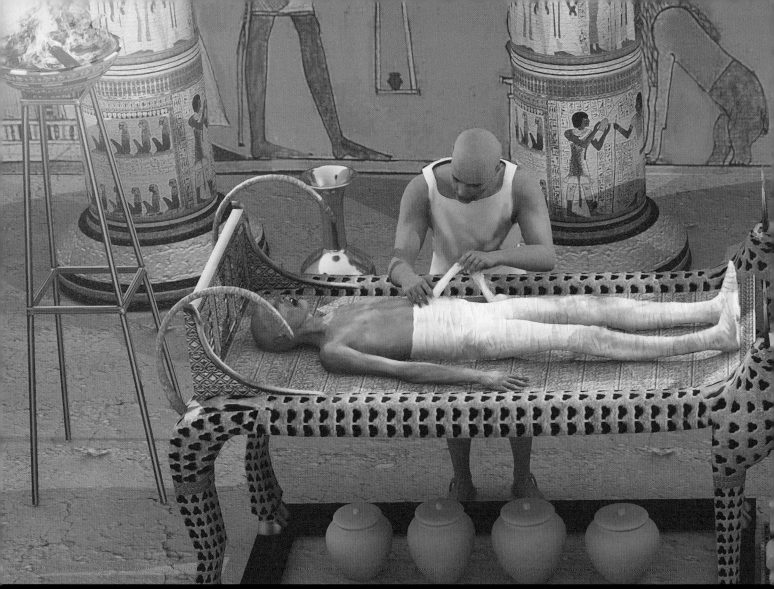

Ancient Egyptians believed in life after death

To ensure **immortality** after death the ancient Egyptians had a set of funeral practices. These included **mummifying** the body, magic spells and burial in a tomb along with the everyday objects that they would need in the afterlife.

To preserve the body the internal organs, apart from the heart, were removed and put into **canopic jars**. The

14

*A priest wraps a dehydrated body in linen. A second body is dried out in natron while a painted **sarcophagus** arrives, ready for a mummy.*

body was then dried out with **natron**. After 40 days it was wrapped in layers of linen with small **amulets** inserted to guard against evil. After this it was coated in resin and placed in a human-shaped coffin.

The ancient Egyptians also mummified animals such as cats, dogs, birds, crocodiles, and baboons.

15

The ancient Egyptians built giant tombs

When the pharaohs of ancient Egypt died their mummified bodies were buried in great tombs with their belongings. Some of the tombs were built as giant pyramids. When finished their shiny white limestone surfaces could be seen glowing in the desert.

A workforce of 10,000 laborers worked in three-month shifts when the Nile flooded. Large blocks of stone were

Blocks of stone cut for the pyramid are hauled on sledges by teams of workers. Each block weighed about 2.5 tons (2.3 metric tons).

cut from quarries and dragged to the building site. Workers lived in specially constructed towns which had sleeping quarters, bakeries, breweries, kitchens, a hospital and a cemetery.

The largest pyramids took around 30 years to build. They are still standing today but their limestone surfaces have worn away.

Priests carried boats during religious festivals

**P**ublic religious ceremonies were very important to the ancient Egyptians. People from all levels of society were involved as they feasted over several days. Free bread and beer was often handed out during these holidays.

The public was excluded from the daily worship of gods in the temples. Only priests tended the statues of

*Crowds gather to see the entombed statue of a god being carried on a boat through the streets during the **Opet Festival**.*

the gods inside. On religious holidays the statues of the gods, entombed and placed on gilded boats, were carried through the streets by priests. The boats were then towed along the Nile River to a temple before making the return trip.

In ancient Egyptian mythology boats were the heavenly transport of the gods.

The ancient Egyptians worshipped many gods

The ancient Egyptians believed in a large group of gods. The gods were involved in all aspects of the people's lives and the natural world around them. These gods and goddesses included important creation **deities** as well as many minor local gods and demons.

Temples were reserved for priests so ordinary people

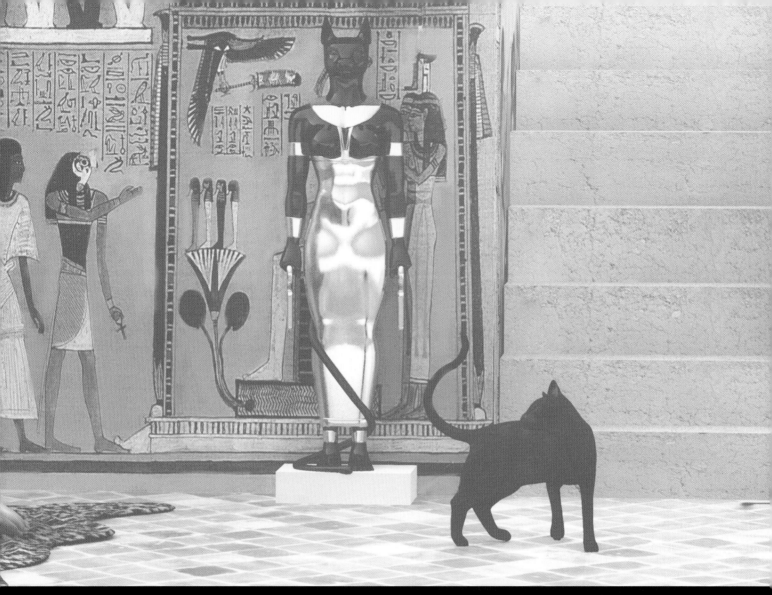

A woman prays to Bastet in a private shrine, leaving an offering of birds and flowers. Bastet was the goddess of cats, joy, dance, music and love.

went to local chapels. Private **shrines** also existed in some homes. People prayed to a god or goddess and left offerings. These were often mummified animals such as birds and cats.

The gods and goddesses of ancient Egypt each took a different form.

Amun Ptah Anubis Osiris Horus Set Thoth Isis Hathor Sobek Ra

21

The ancient Egyptians loved partying

The ancient Egyptians enjoyed having a good time. Entertainment, music, food and drink were a major part of their lives. They celebrated different events throughout the year, such as the harvest, marriages, childbirth and even funerals.

Tomb paintings often show wealthy ancient Egyptians enjoying themselves at banquets where musicians,

Musicians play music while an exotic dancer performs in front of nobles during a day's festivities.

dancers and acrobats perform. Rich dishes of butter, cheese, fowl, and beef, flavored with spices and sweetened with honey and figs, were washed down with beer and wine.

Partygoers wore perfumed wax cones on their heads. These would gradually melt during the party, giving off beautiful scents.

The ancient Egyptians lived in large families

Wealthy ancient Egyptians often had several children. Many died before they grew up. A girl lived at home until she was married at between 15 and 19 years old. She would then move to her husband's house. A boy married at around 20 years old and continued to live in his parents' house with his wife.

A noble family relaxes at home by the garden pool. A daughter plays with her pet as her brother stops playing with his toy cat to chase a bee.

Poorer Egyptians lived in crowded villages. An entire family might live in one room of a house. The other rooms would be home to other families.

In both wealthy and poor families a brother and sister might marry each other. Tutankhamun married his half sister, Ankhesenpaaten.

Ancient Egyptian artisans were highly skilled

Artisans worked alongside others in workshops. They were often well respected, highly trained, and skilled laborers. Their social standing depended on their skills and experience. A few had very comfortable lifestyles.

Objects for temples or the pharaoh were made in the temple or palace workshops. Objects for ordinary people

In a small town workshop, daughters of a wealthy craftsman help decorate various objects, from statues of gods to furniture and pots.

were made by local artisans in small workshops. Artisans included architects, artists, stoneworkers, potters, jewelers, painters, textile workers, dyers and ironsmiths.

Ancient Egyptian artisans produced highly detailed jewelry. This solar scarab pendant was found in Tutankhamun's tomb.

Cleopatra was one of the last pharaohs

 **I**n 332 BC, Egypt was conquered by **Alexander the Great**. After he died one of his closest companions, Ptolemy, became ruler. He founded the Ptolemaic dynasty that was to rule Egypt for nearly 300 years. Cleopatra VII, the last of the Ptolemaic line, became sole ruler of Egypt with the help of two Romans, **Julius Caesar** and, later, **Mark Antony**.

Cleopatra welcomes one of the Roman rulers, Mark Antony, to the Egyptian court.

Cleopatra had children with both Romans and made Caesar's son, Caesarion, co-ruler in name. After Mark Antony was defeated in battle by another Roman, **Octavian**, Cleopatra killed herself.

After the death of Cleopatra in 30 BC, Octavian made the Ptolemaic Kingdom of Egypt part of the Roman Empire.

29

GLOSSARY

Alexander the Great
A Greek king and great military leader who created one of the largest empires of the ancient world.

amulets
Objects that have magical powers of protection.

Antony, Mark

A Roman politician and general who supported Julius Caesar.

Caesar, Julius
A Roman statesman and general who was assassinated in 44 BC.

canopic jars
Storage jars used to preserve the internal organs of a body during the mummification process.

courtiers
High-ranking people who attend royal courts as advisers or companions to the pharaoh.

deities
Gods and goddesses.

dignitaries
People of high rank.

dynasty
A line of rulers that are from the same family.

immortality
The ability to live forever and never die.

mercenaries
A person who is not a member of a country that is at war but fights for them for payment.

mummifying
A process of preserving a person's or animal's body so that it does not decay.

natron
A naturally occurring salty substance which had many uses in ancient Egypt, including drying out bodies during mummification.

Octavian
Later known as Augustus, he was heir to Julius Caesar and the founder of the Roman Empire. He became its first Emperor.

Opet Festival
An ancient Egyptian festival celebrated each year. Statues of the gods Amun, Mut and Khonsu were carried by boat from a temple of Amun in Karnak, to the temple of Luxor.

papyrus
A plant from which paper, reed boats, rope, sandals and baskets were made.

pharaoh
The common title of the kings of ancient Egypt.

prowess
Skill or expertise.

sarcophagus
A funeral box that holds a corpse. In ancient Egypt it could be made in the shape of a human body.

shrines
A sacred place which is dedicated to a specific god or goddess. People worship the god or goddess there.

vizier
A high-ranking political adviser who was second in command to the pharaoh.

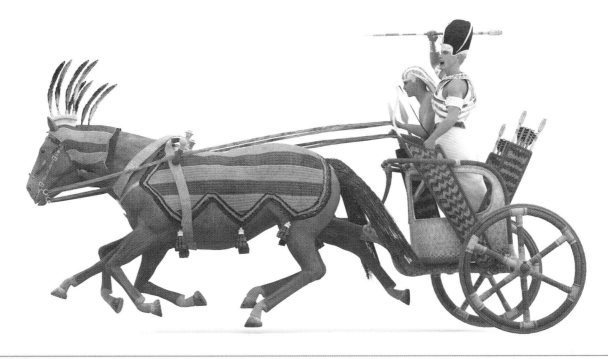

INDEX

FOR MORE INFORMATION

BOOKS

Boyer, Crispin. *National Geographic Kids Everything Ancient Egypt*. Washington, DC: National Geographic, 2012.

Minute Help Guides. *A Kid's Guide to Ancient Egypt*. Minute Help Press, 2013.

WEBSITES

History for Kids – Understanding Ancient Egypt
www.historyforkids.net/ancient-egypt.html

National Geographic Kids – Ten Facts about Ancient Egypt
www.ngkids.co.uk/history/ten-facts-about-ancient-egypt